the POWER of ONE
Every Act of Kindness Counts

by
TRUDY LUDWIG

illustrated by
MIKE CURATO

Alfred A. Knopf ⤳ New York

Sometimes One can feel like
a small and lonely number.

But don't let this little number fool you.

One is a lot bigger and more powerful than you think.

One, after all, is the starting point for change.

One good listener . . .

can make even the smallest voice heard.

One shy smile . . .

can lead to a friendship.

One caring friend . . .

can open the door for several more.

One sincere apology . . .

can help heal big and little hurts.

One warm hug . . .

can lift our spirits up when we're feeling down.

One thoughtful idea . . .

can bring a community together.

One handful of seeds . . .

can sprout into a garden.

One harvested garden . . .

can make a bountiful feast.

Acts and words of kindness do count.

And it all starts with One.

Planting Seeds of Kindness in Your Community

Every year I speak to thousands of students, teachers, and parents in school communities, sharing with them this one basic truth: You don't have to be a superhero with extraordinary powers to be a real hero in someone else's eyes. You can be any kid. You can be an average grown-up like me. All it takes is just one person to reach out in kind ways to make a positive difference in the lives of those we touch. And those acts of kindness can be as simple and straightforward as . . .

- Acknowledging others' presence, so they don't feel invisible
- Saying kind words, whether you're talking to someone face to face or talking about them to someone else
- Including the excluded in your group, game, or activity
- Standing up to put-downs
- Having the courage to take responsibility for intentional/unintentional wrongdoing by apologizing and making up for the hurt you've caused others
- Helping to serve the underserved

Humans are social beings. We all have the fundamental need to belong and feel connected to and valued by our peers. The more seeds of kindness we plant and nurture, the more likely they are to take root and spread—modeling for even more children and adults how they, too, can reach out in supportive ways to connect and improve their relationships with one another and their communities.

Trudy Ludwig

Recommended Books for Young Readers

Boelts, Maribeth. *Those Shoes*. Somerville, MA: Candlewick Press, 2009.

De la Peña, Matt. *Last Stop on Market Street*. New York: G.P. Putnam's Sons, 2015.

DiOrio, Rana. *What Does It Mean to Be Kind?* San Francisco: Little Pickle Press, 2015.

Ludwig, Trudy. *Gifts from the Enemy*. Ashland, OR: White Cloud Press, 2014.

Ludwig, Trudy. *The Invisible Boy*. New York: Alfred A. Knopf Books for Young Readers, 2013.

McCloud, Carol. *Have You Filled a Bucket Today?* Brighton, MI: Bucket Fillers, 2015.

Miller, Pat Zietlow. *Be Kind*. New York: Roaring Brook Press, 2018.

Otoshi, Kathryn. *One*. San Rafael, CA: KO Kids Books, 2008.

Palacio, R. J. *Wonder*. New York: Alfred A. Knopf Books for Young Readers, 2012.

Penfold, Alexandra. *All Are Welcome*. New York: Alfred A. Knopf Books for Young Readers, 2018.

Seuss, Dr. *Horton Hears a Who!* New York: Random House Books for Young Readers, 1954.

Stead, Philip C. *A Sick Day for Amos McGee*. New York: Roaring Brook Press, 2010.

Woodson, Jacqueline. *Each Kindness*. New York: Nancy Paulsen Books, 2012.

Recommended Websites

Ben's Bells helps inspire individuals and communities to practice kindness in their daily lives. bensbells.org

The Great Kindness Challenge empowers students and families to create a culture of kindness by performing as many kind acts as possible. thegreatkindnesschallenge.com

Kids for Peace is an international nonprofit organization focused on youth leadership, community service, and global friendship. kidsforpeaceglobal.org

Life Vest Inside helps empower people to engage in acts of love and kindness. lifevestinside.com

Random Acts of Kindness Foundation provides tips, tools, and resources to promote kindness in school communities and beyond. randomactsofkindness.org

Ripple Kindness Project, based in Australia, offers kindness lessons and activities for young students. ripplekindness.org

The World Kindness Movement is an international movement that fosters goodwill and collaborations in kindness on a global level. theworldkindnessmovement.org

This One is for you, Craig and Jude, with love —T.J.L.

For Christine, one good listener —M.C.

THIS IS A BORZOI BOOK PUBLISHED BY ALFRED A. KNOPF

Text copyright © 2020 by Trudy Ludwig

Jacket art and interior illustrations copyright © 2020 by Mike Curato

All rights reserved. Published in the United States by Alfred A. Knopf, an imprint of Random House
Children's Books, a division of Penguin Random House LLC, New York.

Knopf, Borzoi Books, and the colophon are registered trademarks of Penguin Random House LLC.

Visit us on the Web! rhcbooks.com

Educators and librarians, for a variety of teaching tools,
visit us at RHTeachersLibrarians.com

Library of Congress Cataloging-in-Publication Data is available upon request.

ISBN 978-1-5247-7158-4 (trade) — ISBN 978-1-5247-7159-1 (lib. bdg.) — ISBN 978-1-5247-7160-7 (ebook)

The illustrations in this book were created using pencil, colored pencil, gouache,
watercolor, paper, digital color, and photo collage.

MANUFACTURED IN CHINA

August 2020   10 9 8 7 6 5 4 3 2 1   First Edition